The following illustrations are originally drawn by Mary Louisa Molesworth. She was an English writer of children's stories, in the early 1900s, under the pen name of Mrs Molesworth.
The images were originally published throughout the books she wrote.

If you find this coloring book relaxing or entertaining, please keep an eye out for further public domain coloring books by Kaden Stillwell.

The images in this coloring are public domain! However, I did take some time to clean them up and make them nice enough to color.

'Can I——?' he began, then hesitated.   p. 23.

"—Oh Ruby!" she suddenly broke off, 'do look here — oh, how love -ly!' P. 60

'Mavis,' said the soft yet clear and thril-
ling voice, 'you see me, my child?'
P. 81.

'Winfried drew forward a chair; in another minute he had reached down the cross.' p. 125.

'—Bertrand—look—where is Mavis—Mavis and the boat; can you see them?'

P·148·

"Are—— are you a mermaid, or a that other thing?" asked the child." P. 156.

"Stop a moment," said the boy. "Stop and listen—hush—there now, do you hear them ringing?" p. 172.

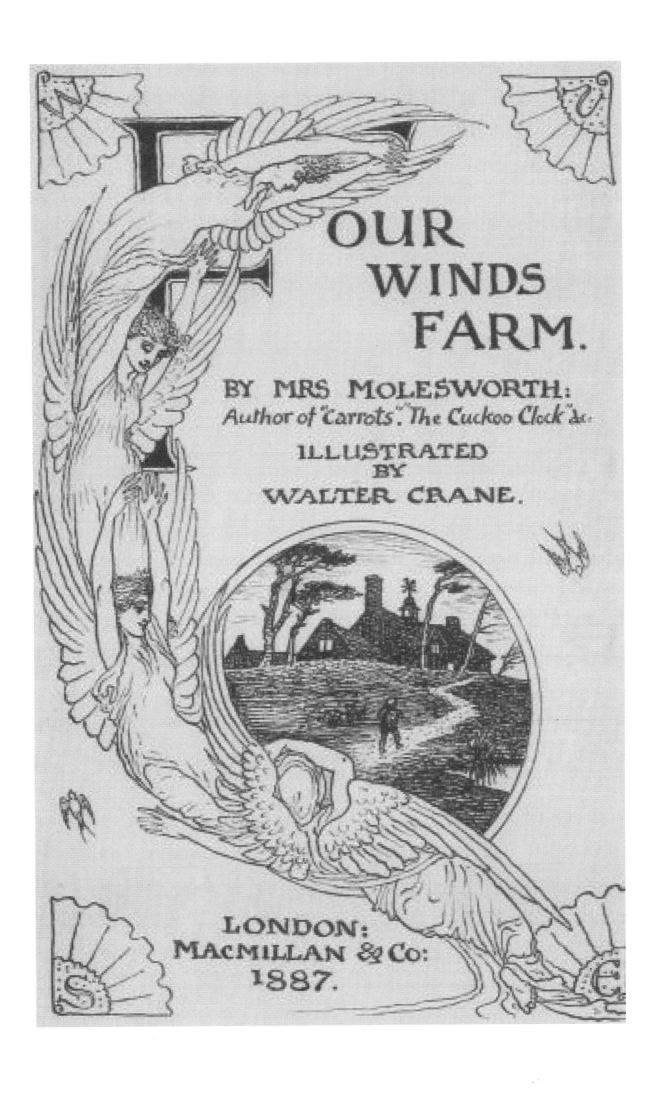

FOUR
WINDS
FARM.

BY MRS MOLESWORTH:
Author of "Carrots": "The Cuckoo Clock" &c.

ILLUSTRATED
BY
WALTER CRANE.

LONDON:
MACMILLAN & Co:
1887.

p 52

p 92

LITTLE MISS PEGGY:

ONLY A NURSERY STORY BY

MRS. MOLESWORTH

WITH PICTURES BY
WALTER CRANE

LONDON:
MACMILLAN & CO.
AND NEW YORK
1887

Made in the USA
Columbia, SC
12 December 2021

51207334R00080